W9-CSB-559

The Child's World®

Published by The Child's World®
1980 Lookout Drive • Mankato, MN 56003-1705
800-599-READ • www.childsworld.com

ACKNOWLEDGMENTS
The Child's World®: Mary Berendes, Publishing Director
The Design Lab: Design
Jody Jensen Shaffer: Editing
Pamela J. Mitsakos: Photo Research

PHOTO CREDITS
DieterMeyrl/iStock.com: 14; gorillaimages/Shutterstock.com: cover, 1, 18;
In Green /Shutterstock.com: 21; Konstantin Shishkin/Shutterstock.com: 13;
Mayovskyy Andrew/Shutterstock.com: 5; MICHELANGELOBOY/iStock.
com:10; nialat/Shutterstock.com: 17; Peky/Shutterstock.com: 6; Richard
Susanto/Shutterstock: 22; Sunny Forest/Shutterstock.com: 9

ISBN 9781626870284
LCCN 2013947393

Printed in the United States of America in Mankato, Minnesota.
November 2013
PA02200

ABOUT THE AUTHORS

Cynthia Amoroso has worked as an elementary school teacher and a high school English teacher. Writing children's books is another way for her to share her passion for the written word.

Robert B. Noyed has worked as a newspaper reporter and in the communications department for a Minnesota school district. He enjoys the challenge and accomplishment of writing children's books.

Winter

BY CYNTHIA AMOROSO AND ROBERT B. NOYED

Winter is here! Winter is one of the four **seasons**. It comes after fall and before spring.

Winter is the first season of the year.

Winter is not the same everywhere. In some places, winter can be very cold. In other places, winter is warmer.

Deserts are warmer than the plains in the winter.

When winter is cold, it can
bring snow. When it snows,
the ground and the trees
become covered in white.

This forest is covered in snow.

Big storms can bring lots of snow. Strong winds blow the snow. These storms are called **blizzards**.

It can be hard to see through the snow during a blizzard.

The cold winter air **freezes** water. A **layer** of ice forms on the tops of ponds and lakes.

In the winter, a layer of ice forms on lakes.

Winter can be a hard time for animals. It is not easy to find food. Some animals, such as bears, sleep through much of the winter.

A bear gets ready to sleep for the winter.

Some animals grow **thick** fur in the winter. This fur helps them stay warm.

Rabbits grow more fur in the winter.

Many people enjoy being outdoors during winter. Skiing is a favorite winter sport. It is fun to ice skate, too.

These children are skiing in the mountains.

Children play in the snow.

They like to make snowmen.

They slide down hills on sleds.

A snowman is made from three giant snowballs.

Winter is the coldest season.
Snow is falling all around.
Have fun out in the snow!

What do you like to do in the snow?

Glossary

blizzards (BLIZ-urdz): Blizzards are big snowstorms. Blizzards bring lots of snow.

freezes (FREEZ-ez): If something freezes, it turns from a liquid to a solid. Water freezes to form ice.

layer (LAY-ur): A layer is a coating on something. A layer of ice forms over lakes in the winter.

seasons (SEE-zinz): Seasons are the four parts of the year. The four seasons are winter, spring, summer, and fall.

thick (THIK): If something is thick, it has many parts close together. In the winter, animals grow thick fur.

To Find Out More

Books

Branley, Franklyn M. *Sunshine Makes the Seasons*. New York: HarperCollins, 2005.

Owen, Ruth. *How Do You Know It's Winter?* New York: Bearport, 2012.

Rockwell, Anne. *Four Seasons Make a Year*. New York: Walker & Co., 2004.

Web Sites

Visit our Web site for links about winter: *childsworld.com/links*

Note to Parents, Teachers, and Librarians: We routinely verify our Web links to make sure they are safe and active sites. So encourage your readers to check them out!

Index